T0221894

## RAVENPAW'S PATH

### #2: A CLAN IN NEED

# WARRIORS
## RAVENPAW'S PATH
### #2: A CLAN IN NEED

CREATED BY
**ERIN HUNTER**

WRITTEN BY
**DAN JOLLEY**

ART BY
**JAMES L. BARRY**

HAMBURG // LONDON // LOS ANGELES // TOKYO

**HARPER**
*An Imprint of* HarperCollins*Publishers*

## Warriors: Ravenpaw's Path Vol. 2:
## A Clan in Need
### Created by Erin Hunter
### Written by Dan Jolley
### Art by James L. Barry

Digital Tones - Lincy Chan
Lettering - John Hunt
Cover Design - Louis Csontos

Editor - Lillian Diaz-Przybyl
Managing Editor - Vy Nguyen
Print-Production Manager - Lucas Rivera
Art Director - Al-Insan Lashley
Director of Sales and Manufacturing - Allyson DeSimone
Associate Publisher - Marco Pavia
President and C.O.O. - John Parker
C.E.O. and Chief Creative Officer - Stu Levy

A 🐝 **TOKYOPOP** Manga

TOKYOPOP and 🐝 are trademarks or registered trademarks of TOKYOPOP Inc.

TOKYOPOP Inc.
5900 Wilshire Blvd. Suite 2000
Los Angeles, CA 90036

E-mail: info@TOKYOPOP.com
Come visit us online at www.TOKYOPOP.com

ISBN 978-0-06-168866-9
Library of Congress catalog card number: 2009921414

23 24 25 26 27 LBC 20 19 18 17 16
❖
First Edition

Hello!

I always say that no character in Warriors is based on me, but if pushed, I'd have to admit that Ravenpaw has the most in common with my personality. We're both a little awkward in social situations, and happier with just one or two people around. Put it this way, if I lost my home tomorrow, I'd head for a cozy barn just like Barley's! Revisiting Ravenpaw and Barley in their manga trilogy has been a great treat for me, because in my imagination their story always carried on, even when they had left the pages of the main series.

One of the best things about the manga is that we can recall characters who appeared fleetingly in earlier books and bring them to the front and center of the action. In this story, Barley's history with BloodClan returns to haunt him. After Scourge was killed in *The Darkest Hour*, the remaining BloodClan cats scattered. But they only ran away as far as the Twolegplace, which meant there were plenty of opportunities for new leaders to rise. . . .

Poor Barley, he tried so hard to put his old life behind him. I think he would have ignored it even longer if it wasn't for his sister, Violet, who couldn't forget what had happened—and more to the point, still wanted revenge. It would be too easy to write about cats who leaped into battle at the first sign of trouble; what is more interesting to me is to watch how cats who don't want to fight are persuaded to change their minds. Barley becomes a hero in this book; think of it as my way of celebrating the cats (or people) who choose to walk alone, yet still have the courage to take on the shadows from their past.

Best wishes always,
Erin Hunter

THIS WHOLE EXPERIENCE SEEMS LIKE A DREAM TO ME.

GETTING DRIVEN OUT OF THE FARM...COMING HERE TO THE MOONSTONE...SEEING STARCLAN IN A DREAM...

THE CLOSER WE GET TO THUNDERCLAN TERRITORY, THE MORE EXCITED I GET. IT'S LIKE A HOMECOMING, SORT OF.

HEY! LET'S GO TO THE CAMP BY WAY OF FOURTREES!

I CAN SHOW YOU WHAT THE GATHERING SPOT IS LIKE WHEN IT'S NOT COVERED UP WITH A BUNCH OF FIGHTING CATS.

UH...YEAH, OKAY.

SEE? ISN'T THIS PLACE GREAT?

I GUESS SO.

AND THERE'S THE GREAT ROCK!

ONCE EVERY FULL MOON, THE CLAN LEADERS STAND UP THERE TO ADDRESS ALL THE CATS.

MMM-HMM.

SKRRTCH
SKRRTCH

HEY-- DO YOU HEAR THAT?

LET ME GUESS.

CROWKIT, RIGHT?

OH--HI!

YOU MIND TELLING US WHAT IT IS YOU'RE DOING, EXACTLY?

I WANT TO SEE WHAT IT'S LIKE TO BE A LEADER! BUT, UH...

...I CAN'T CLIMB THE ROCK.

WHO ARE THEY?

I'VE NEVER SEEN THEM BEFORE!

THAT'S RAVENPAW AND BARLEY. THEY'RE ROGUES, BUT THEY'RE THE BEST KIND OF ROGUES.

THEY HELPED THUNDERCLAN WHEN WE NEEDED IT THE MOST.

WOW...

YOU'VE HAD LITTLE ONES! THEY'RE BEAUTIFUL!

YOU AND FIRESTAR MUST BE SO PROUD!

*I RECOGNIZE FIRESTAR'S MATE, SANDSTORM, AT ONCE. BUT THOSE KITS WITH HER...*

THAT WE ARE, OLD FRIEND.

SEEMS LIKE ONLY YESTERDAY THAT YOU AND I WERE THAT YOUNG, DOESN'T IT?

RAVENPAW, WELCOME BACK!

LIFE ON THE FARM MUST BE AGREEING WITH YOU.

WELL...

BARLEY, WELCOME TO THUNDERCLAN.

THANK YOU, FIRESTAR.

EVERYTHING SEEMS RIGHT HERE. ESPECIALLY WITH FIRESTAR. THE CATS ALL LOVE HIM.

ARE YOU HUNGRY? THERE'S ENOUGH TO SHARE.

FIRESTAR OBVIOUSLY WANTS TO PUT US AT EASE.

I DECIDE NOT TO BRING UP OUR TROUBLES UNTIL HE'S READY.

WAS I WRONG TO ASK, FIRESTAR?

NO.

WE'LL DO WHAT WE CAN.

NOW YOU MUST REST IN OUR CAMP.

32

I WAIT A FEW MINUTES FOR THE PANIC TO DIE DOWN BEFORE I TRY TO FIGURE ANYTHING OUT.

FIRESTAR?

WHAT'S GOING ON? WHAT HAPPENED TO YOUR PATROL?

CATS HAVE BEEN COMING FROM TWOLEGPLACE. LAUNCHING RAIDS ON THUNDERCLAN TERRITORY.

ATTACKING THUNDERCLAN PATROLS AND STEALING PREY.

I HAD HOPED THE TROUBLE WITH TWOLEGPLACE ROGUES WOULD HAVE STOPPED, NOW THAT SCOURGE IS DEAD...

...BUT IT HASN'T. AND THESE RAIDS ARE GETTING MORE FREQUENT.

TWO STRONG WARRIORS, GRAYSTRIPE AND CLOUDTAIL, ARE READY TO GO AND WAITING FOR US.

OF COURSE, SOME OF US ARE MORE READY TO GO THAN OTHERS. I DON'T THINK BARLEY'S EVER HAD TO WAKE UP THIS EARLY.

COME ON, BARLEY, LET'S GO! THEY'RE WAITING!

JUS' LEMME SLEEP A LITTLE MORE. JUS' A LITTLE SNOOZE.

GET UP!

36

IT'S A SUCCESSFUL PATROL. WE'VE GOT A DAY'S WORTH OF FRESH-KILL...

...AND WE'RE STARTING TO THINK EVERYTHING'S GOING TO BE QUIET.

WE'RE MISTAKEN ABOUT THAT.

BUT THEN--RIGHT IN THE MIDDLE OF EVERYTHING--

--SOMETHING STRANGE HAPPENS.

BARLEY REACTS AS IF THE CAT WITH THE TORN EAR HADN'T SAID ANYTHING AT ALL...

HEY!

HEY! YOU!

AND IT TURNS OUT I WASN'T THE ONLY ONE WHO NOTICED, EITHER.

DID YOU KNOW THOSE CATS?

...NO. NO, I DIDN'T.

REALLY? BECAUSE THEY SEEMED TO KNOW YOU.

GRAYSTRIPE DOESN'T GET THE CHANCE TO KEEP ASKING BARLEY QUESTIONS.

MEW!

!

?

BUT I CAN TELL HE'S NOT FINISHED WITH THIS.

"THOSE CATS BACK THERE..."

...YOU KNEW THEM WHEN YOU WERE IN BLOODCLAN, DIDN'T YOU?

THAT PART OF MY LIFE IS OVER.

I DON'T WANT TO TALK ABOUT IT.

I KNOW HOW MUCH BARLEY HAS SUFFERED BECAUSE OF BLOODCLAN. IF HE DOESN'T WANT TO TALK, I'M NOT GOING TO PRESSURE HIM.

IT'S NOT JUST ME INVOLVED, THOUGH.

BARLEY.

MAY WE SPEAK WITH YOU?

THAT SHOULDER GOING TO BE ALL RIGHT?

I HOPE SO. IT'S PRETTY STIFF.

WHERE'S THE FOOD, SANDSTORM? WE'RE HUNGRY!

CAN'T WE HAVE AT LEAST A MOUSE?

I'M SORRY, KITS. WE HAVE TO MAKE DO WITHOUT TODAY.

*I CAN HEAR THE PAIN AND HUNGER FROM THE CAMP. I KNOW BARLEY CAN, TOO.*

I KNOW WHAT BLOODCLAN DID TO YOU. BUT THESE ARE MY FRIENDS.

CAN WE REALLY LET THEM SUFFER?

THE NEXT DAY COMES, ALONG WITH THE CRYING OF KITS AND THE RUMBLING OF EMPTY BELLIES.

AND BARLEY STILL MIGHT AS WELL BE MADE OF STONE, FOR ALL THE NOISE HE MAKES.

DON'T WORRY, SANDSTORM. WE'RE HEADING OUT NOW. I KNOW WHERE THERE'S SOME GOOD HUNTING.

WE'LL HAVE THOSE KITS FED BEFORE YOU KNOW IT.

GOOD LUCK, YOU TWO!

THAT NIGHT, FIRESTAR CALLS A COUNCIL OF ALL THE CLAN WARRIORS, AND EVERYONE LISTENS HARD TO WHAT BARLEY HAS TO SAY.

I KNOW HOW DIFFICULT THIS IS FOR HIM. I'M SO PROUD OF HIM FOR DOING IT!

THOSE WERE BLOODCLAN CATS THAT ATTACKED US, BUT IT'S MORE THAN THAT.

THEY WERE SOME OF SCOURGE'S CLOSEST ADVISORS.

BUT I'M PRETTY SURE BARLEY
HATES IT EVEN MORE THAN I DO.

I WANT TO GET CAUGHT UP, VIOLET, I REALLY DO. BUT WE HAVE SOMETHING IMPORTANT WE HAVE TO ASK YOU.

*BARLEY FILLS HER IN ON EVERYTHING THAT'S HAPPENED AS QUICKLY AS HE CAN. I HATE TO SEE HER HAPPINESS FADE SO FAST.*

I'VE BEEN HEARING RUMORS ABOUT EX-BLOODCLAN CATS GETTING TOGETHER. THEY SAY THEY'RE GETTING ORGANIZED AGAIN.

MY FRIENDS AND I DON'T LEAVE OUR YARDS MUCH, BUT...WORD GETS AROUND. AND--

--SOMETIMES, DOWN THE ALLEYS, I THINK I CAN HEAR FIGHTING.

IT WAS MUCH BETTER AFTER SCOURGE WENT, BUT IT STARTED TO GET BAD AGAIN ABOUT A MOON AGO.

IS THERE ONE CAT IN CHARGE? WHERE DOES HE LIVE?

I DON'T KNOW, BUT I CAN FIND OUT. NO MORE CATS SHOULD SUFFER!

*VIOLET IS IMPRESSIVE. SHE'S SO BRAVE, AND POSITIVE!*

*IT TOOK BARLEY SO LONG TO WORK UP THIS KIND OF COURAGE, BUT SHE'S READY TO GO, ON THE SPOT.*

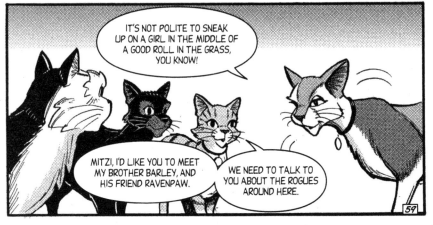

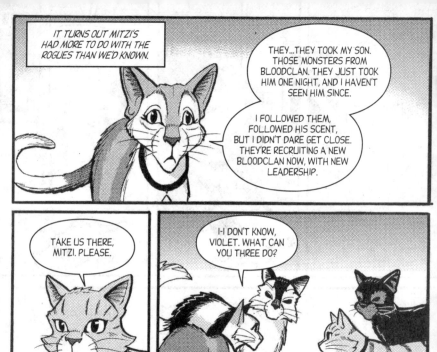

IT TURNS OUT MITZI'S HAD MORE TO DO WITH THE ROGUES THAN WE'D KNOWN.

THEY...THEY TOOK MY SON. THOSE MONSTERS FROM BLOODCLAN. THEY JUST TOOK HIM ONE NIGHT, AND I HAVEN'T SEEN HIM SINCE.

I FOLLOWED THEM, FOLLOWED HIS SCENT, BUT I DIDN'T DARE GET CLOSE. THEY'RE RECRUITING A NEW BLOODCLAN NOW, WITH NEW LEADERSHIP.

TAKE US THERE, MITZI. PLEASE.

MAYBE WE CAN FIND YOUR SON.

I-I DON'T KNOW, VIOLET. WHAT CAN YOU THREE DO?

IT WON'T BE JUST US. IF WE CAN FIND OUT WHERE THESE CATS LIVE, THERE ARE MORE WHO WOULD FIGHT THEM, TOO.

A LOT MORE.

WITH MITZI CONVINCED, WE SET OUT... AND THE CLOSER WE GOT TO THIS PLACE, EVEN THOUGH I HADN'T SEEN IT YET, THE TENSER I GOT.

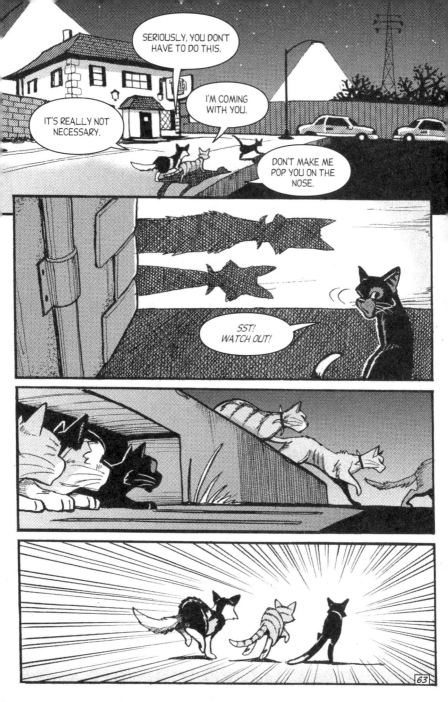

YOU ARE THE NEXT GENERATION.

YOU ARE THE ONES CHOSEN FOR THIS.

AND WE ARE THE ONES WHO WILL GIVE YOU EVERYTHING YOU DESERVE...

69

...IN EXCHANGE FOR YOUR ABSOLUTE LOYALTY.

READY...ON MY SIGNAL....

VIOLET?

WHAT ARE YOU DOING?

HOOT!

JUMPER!

THE SILENCE IN THIS PLACE IS SO SUDDEN, AND SO PROFOUND...

...I THINK I CAN ACTUALLY HEAR THESE ROGUES' ATTITUDES CHANGING.

WAIT! WAIT!

IT'S JUMPER AND HOOT! REMEMBER US?

WE'RE KIN, LIKE YOU SAID! YOU WOULDN'T HURT YOUR OLD LITTERMATES, WOULD YOU?

BARLEY...

PROTECT US, BROTHER...!

AND WITH THAT, HOOT AND JUMPER WERE GONE.....

A FEW TERRIFIED ROGUES WERE STILL MILLING AROUND BUT THERE WAS ONE IN PARTICULAR WE'D FORGOTTEN ABOUT.

EXCUSE ME..... VI- VIOLET?

WHAT? YOU ROGUES HAVEN'T HAD ENOUGH?

NO! I MEAN...YES. VIOLET, IT'S FRITZ. I USED TO LIVE NEXT DOOR!

YOU'RE MITZI'S SON! ARE YOU OKAY? DID THEY HURT YOU?

THEY BROUGHT ME HERE A MOON AGO AND WOULDN'T LET ME LEAVE! THEY TRIED TO MAKE ME JOIN BLOODCLAN AND TEACH ME TO FIGHT...

BUT I'M NO GOOD AT THAT. I JUST WANT TO GO HOME.

I KNOW THE FEELING...

OH, FRITZ... WE'LL GET YOU HOME. MITZI WILL BE SO HAPPY!

WARRIORS-- WE'RE DONE HERE.

IT'S TIME TO LEAVE.

WELL...I SUPPOSE IT'S TIME FOR US TO GO BACK TO OUR LIVES NOW.

I'M GLAD YOU HAVE A HOME WHERE YOU CAN BE SAFE AND HAPPY.

ALL RIGHT...WELL, I'LL TAKE VIOLET BACK TO HER PLACE, THEN COME BACK TO THUNDERCLAN.

OH--I'LL GO WITH YOU.

NO...NO, THAT'S NOT NECESSARY.

I'LL TAKE HER HOME ON MY OWN.

"SO LET'S GO TAKE IT BACK!"

TO BE CONCLUDED

# ERIN
# HUNTER

is inspired by a love of cats and a fascination with the ferocity of the natural world. As well as having great respect for nature in all its forms, Erin enjoys creating rich, mythical explanations for animal behavior. She is also the author of the bestselling Seekers series.

Visit the Clans online
and play Warriors games at
www.warriorcats.com.

For exclusive information on your favorite authors and artists, visit
www.authortracker.com.

The #1 national bestselling series, now in manga!

# WARRIORS

## RAVENPAW'S PATH

### THE HEART OF A WARRIOR

TOKYOPOP

HARPER COLLINS

ERIN HUNTER

# WARRIORS

## RAVENPAW'S PATH

### #3: THE HEART
### OF A WARRIOR

Ravenpaw and Barley helped their friends in Thunder-
Clan defeat the vicious BloodClan cats in Twolegplace,
and now they're ready to fight to reclaim their home
on the farm. Firestar has promised to send a warrior
patrol to assist them, but Ravenpaw worries that it
won't be enough to chase out the invaders. He knows
that he must find his courage and fight like a warrior—
or lose his home forever.

# WARRIORS

## THE LOST WARRIOR

## WARRIOR'S REFUGE

## WARRIOR'S RETURN

Find out what really happened to Graystripe when he was captured by Twolegs, and follow him and Millie on their torturous journey through the old forest territory and Twolegplace to find ThunderClan.

# WARRIORS

## TIGERSTAR AND SASHA

### #1: INTO THE WOODS

### #2: ESCAPE FROM THE FOREST

### #3: RETURN TO THE CLANS

Sasha has everything she wants: kind housefolk who take care of her during the day and the freedom to explore the woods beyond Twolegplace at night. But when Sasha is forced to leave her home, she must forge a solitary new life in the forest. When Sasha meets Tigerstar, leader of ShadowClan, she begins to think that she may be better off joining the ranks of his forest Clan. But Tigerstar has many secrets, and Sasha must decide whether she can trust him.

# WARRIORS

## THE RISE OF SCOURGE

TOKYOPOP®

HARPER COLLINS

# ERIN HUNTER

# WARRIORS

## THE RISE OF
## SCOURGE

Black-and-white Tiny may be the runt of the litter, but he's also the most curious about what lies beyond the backyard fence. When he crosses paths with some wild cats defending their territory, Tiny is left with scars—and a bitter, deep-seated grudge—that he carries with him back to Twolegplace. As his reputation grows among the strays and loners that live in the dirty brick alleyways, Tiny leaves behind his name, his kittypet past, and everything that was once important to him—except his deadly desire for revenge.

THE #1 NATIONAL BESTSELLING SERIES

OMEN OF THE STARS

WARRIORS

FADING ECHOES

ERIN HUNTER

TURN THE PAGE FOR A PEEK AT
THE NEXT WARRIORS NOVEL,

# WARRIORS

## OMEN OF THE STARS #2:
## FADING ECHOES

Three ThunderClan cats, Jayfeather, Lionblaze, and Dovepaw, have been prophesied to hold the power of the stars in their paws. Now they must work together to unravel the meaning behind the ancient words of the prophecy.

As Jayfeather tackles his new responsibilities as the Clan's sole medicine cat, and Lionblaze trains his apprentice in the ways of the warrior cats, Dovepaw hones her own unique ability and tries to use it for the good of ThunderClan. But the dark shadows that have preyed on the Clan for many moons still lurk just beyond the forest. Soon a mysterious visitor will walk in one cat's dreams whispering promises of greatness, with results that will change the future of ThunderClan in ways that no cat could have foreseen.

*Trees whispered, branch to branch,* above the lifeless forest floor. Mist wreathed their smooth trunks, pale as bone, and swirled through the night-dark forest. Above their branches, the sky yawned, starless and cold. There was no moon to cast shadows, but an eerie light glowed through the trees.

Paws thudded on the dead earth. Two warriors reared on their hind legs and launched themselves at each other, their bodies heaving and twisting like ghosts in the gloom. One brown. One black. Wind rattled the trees as the brown tom, his broad shoulders heaving, aimed a vicious swipe at his lean opponent. The black tom dodged, not taking his gaze from his rival's paws for a moment, his eyes narrowed in concentration.

The brown warrior's strike missed and he landed heavily, too slow in turning to avoid a sharp nip from the black tom. Hissing, he reared again, twisted on one hind paw, and lunged, his forepaws falling like rocks on the black tom's shoulders.

The tom collapsed under the weight of the blow. Breath

huffed from his mouth as his chest slammed against the ground. The brown warrior raked thorn-sharp claws along his opponent's pelt, and his nose twitched as blood welled in the wound, scarlet and salty.

Quick as a snake, the black tom slithered out from his rival's grip and began to swipe rhythmically with his forepaws, swaying one way then the other until the brown warrior flinched away. In that flinch—a single moment of distraction—the black tom sprang forward and sank his teeth deep into the warrior's foreleg.

The warrior yowled and shook the tom off, his eyes flaming with rage. A heartbeat passed as the cats stared at each other, both gazes glittering with calculation. Then the black tom ducked and twisted, raking his way under the brown warrior's snow white belly. But the warrior pounced on him before he could scramble clear, hooking his pelt with long, curved claws and pinning him to the ground.

"Too slow," the brown warrior growled.

The black tom struggled, panic flashing in his eyes as his rival's jaws began to close around his throat.

"*Enough.*" A dark tabby stepped from the shadows, his massive paws stirring the mist.

The cats froze, then untangled themselves. The brown warrior sat back on his haunches, one foreleg raised as though it hurt. The black tom scrambled to his paws, spraying droplets of blood across the forest floor as he shook out his fur.

"Some good moves, Hawkfrost." The dark tabby nodded to the broad-shouldered warrior; then his gaze flicked to the black tom. "You're getting better, Breezepelt, but you'll need to be even quicker if you're going to outfight stronger warriors. If you can't match an opponent in weight, look to speed instead and use his weight against him."

Breezepelt dipped his head. "I'll work on it, Tigerstar."

A fourth tom slid from the shadows. His silver stripes gleamed in the half-light as he wound around Tigerstar. "Hawkfrost can match any warrior," he purred, smooth as honey. "There aren't many cats with such skill and strength."

Tigerstar curled his lip. "Quiet, Darkstripe!" he hissed. "Hawkfrost knows his own strengths."

Darkstripe blinked. "I wasn't—"

Tigerstar cut him off. "And there's always room for improvement."

A fifth cat slid from behind a tree, his night-colored pelt ragged against the smooth gray bark. "Hawkfrost depends too much on his strength," he muttered. "Breezepelt too much on his speed. Together they would make a great warrior. Separately they are vulnerable."

"Brokenstar." Hawkfrost greeted the matted tabby with bared teeth. "Are we supposed to take advice from the warrior who failed to silence Jayfeather?"

Brokenstar twitched the tip of his tail. "I did not expect StarClan to fight so hard to save him."

"Never underestimate your enemy." Hawkfrost stretched his forepaw, wincing.

Breezepelt licked the deep scratches along his flank, his tongue reddening with his own blood.

"We must be ready," Tigerstar growled. "It's not enough to be able to beat one enemy at a time. We must train until we can take on a whole patrol single-pawed."

Breezepelt looked up from his wound, his eyes flashing. "I can already beat Harespring and Leaftail in training."

Tigerstar's eyes darkened. "Training is one thing. Warriors fight harder when they're defending their lives."

Breezepelt clawed the ground. "I can fight harder."

Tigerstar nodded. "You have more reason than most."

A growl rose in Breezepelt's throat.

"You have been wronged," Tigerstar meowed softly.

Breezepelt's young face looked kitlike in the gloom. "You're the only ones who seem to realize that."

"I have told you that you must seek vengeance," Tigerstar reminded him. "With our help, you can take revenge on every cat who has betrayed you."

Breezepelt's gaze grew hungry as the dark warrior went on.

"And on every cat who stood by and did nothing while others claimed what was yours as their own."

"Starting with Crowfeather." Breezepelt snarled his father's name.

Brokenstar swished his crooked tail through the air. "What did your father do to defend you?" His words were laced with bitterness, as though soured by his own memories.

Darkstripe slunk forward. "He never valued you."

Tigerstar shooed the striped warrior back with a flick of his tail. "He tried to crush you, make you weak."

"He didn't succeed," Breezepelt spat.

"But he tried. Perhaps he valued his ThunderClan kits more. Those three kits should never have been born." Tigerstar padded toward the young warrior, his eyes gleaming, holding Breezepelt's gaze like a snake mesmerizing its prey. "You have been suckled on lies and the weakness of others. You have suffered while others have thrived. But you are strong. You will put things right. Your father betrayed his Clan and betrayed you. Leafpool betrayed StarClan by taking a mate."

Breezepelt's tail was lashing. "I will make them all pay for what they have done." No heat fired his gaze, only cold hatred. "I will have vengeance on each and every one of them."

Brokenstar pushed forward. "You are a noble warrior, Breezepelt. You cannot live a life spawned on lies. Loyalty to the warrior code runs too strong in your blood."

"Not like those weaklings," Breezepelt agreed.

Hawkfrost was on his paws. "More practice?" he suggested.

Tigerstar shook his head. "There is something else you must do." He swung his broad head around to face the warrior.

Hawkfrost narrowed his eyes to icy slits. "What?"

"There's another apprentice," Tigerstar told him. "She has great power. She must join us to make the battle even."

"You want me to visit her?" Menace edged Hawkfrost's mew.

Tigerstar nodded. "Walk in her dreams. Teach her that our battle is her destiny." He flicked the tip of his long, dark tail. "Go."

As the broad-shouldered warrior turned away and padded into the mist, Tigerstar growled after him, "You should have no trouble. She is ready."